Reader's Clubhouse

SWEET DREAMS

By Marc Tyler Nobleman
Illustrated by Nan Brooks

BARRON'S

D0424114

Table of Contents

Illustration on page 21 by Carol Stutz; Illustrations on pages 22–23 by Deborah Gross

All inquiries should be addressed to:
Barron's Educational Series, Inc.
250 Wireless Boulevard
Hauppauge, New York 11788
www.barronseduc.com

Library of Congress Catalog Card No.: 2006028819

ISBN-13: 978-0-7641-3721-1
ISBN-10: 0-7641-3721-2

Library of Congress Cataloging-in-Publication Data
Nobleman, Marc Tyler
    Sweet dreams / by Marc Tyler Nobleman
        p. cm. — (Reader's clubhouse)
    ISBN-13: 978-0-7641-3721-1
    ISBN-10: 0-7641-3721-2
    1. English language—Phonetics—Juvenile literature. I. Title.

PE1135.N63 2007
 372.46'5—dc22

2006028819

PRINTED IN CHINA
9 8 7 6 5 4 3 2 1

Dear Parent and Educator,

Welcome to the Barron's Reader's Clubhouse, a series of books that provide a phonics approach to reading.

Phonics is the relationship between letters and sounds. It is a system that teaches children that letters have specific sounds. Level 1 books introduce the short-vowel sounds. Level 2 books progress to the long-vowel sounds. Level 3 books then go on to vowel combinations and words ending in "y." This progression matches how phonics is taught in many classrooms.

Sweet Dreams introduces the "ea," "ee," and "ie" vowel combination sound. Simple words with this vowel combination are called **decodable words.** The child knows how to sound out these words because he or she has learned the sound they include. This story also contains **high-frequency words.** These are common, everyday words that the child learns to read by sight. High-frequency words help ensure fluency and comprehension. **Challenging words** go a little beyond the reading level. The child may need help from an adult to understand these words. All words are listed by their category on page 24.

Here are some coaching and prompting statements you can use to help a young reader read *Sweet Dreams:*

- **On page 4, "sweet" is a decodable word. Point to the word and say:**
  Read this word. How did you know the word? What sounds did it make?
  Note: There are many opportunities to repeat the above instruction throughout the book.

- **On page 12, "prairie" is a challenging word. Point to the word and say:**
  Read this word. Sound out the word. How did you know the word? What helped you?

You'll find more coaching ideas on the Reader's Clubhouse Web site: *www.barronsclubhouse.com.* Reader's Clubhouse is designed to teach and reinforce reading skills in a fun way. We hope you enjoy helping children discover their love of reading!

Sincerely,

Nancy Harris

Nancy Harris
Reading Consultant

I love my twin sisters.
Allie and Ellie are funny. They
are sweet.

But they will not go to sleep.

If we do not make a peep,
then you will sleep. Sweet
dreams, Allie and Ellie.

Oh! There is a creak! Don't weep, Allie and Ellie. What can we do to get you to sleep?

Look at this feast! If you eat,
then you will sleep. Sweet
dreams, Allie and Ellie.

Oh! There is a leak! Don't
weep, Allie and Ellie. What can
we do to get you to sleep?

Let's go to the beach. The
sea waves will help put you to
sleep. Sweet dreams, Allie
and Ellie.

Oh! They see the last gleam of the sun. Don't weep, Allie and Ellie. What can we do to get you to sleep?

Let's go to the prairie. The
breeze in the field will put you
to sleep.

Oh! Bees are buzzing around
their beehive. Don't weep, Allie
and Ellie. What can we do to
get you to sleep?

Let's find a house in a tree. As you peek at the leaves, you will go to sleep.

Oh! They see an eagle sixteen feet up. Don't weep, Allie and Ellie. What can we do to get you to sleep?

It is three o'clock. We are back on our street.

We are weak. We are beat. We
did not succeed.

Now we have found a little
peace.

But Allie and Ellie still will not
sleep. Good night, Allie
and Ellie.

Fun Facts About
Sleep

- Your eyes move while you sleep. Some people even sleep with their eyes open.

- Some animals sleep standing up. Elephants and horses sleep standing up.

- Children need about ten hours of sleep per night. This helps them stay healthy. Adults need about six to eight hours of sleep per night.

- A "catnap" is a quick nap. The term came about because cats go to sleep many times during the day.

• Some people have a hard time falling asleep at night. Here are some things you can do to help you get to sleep.

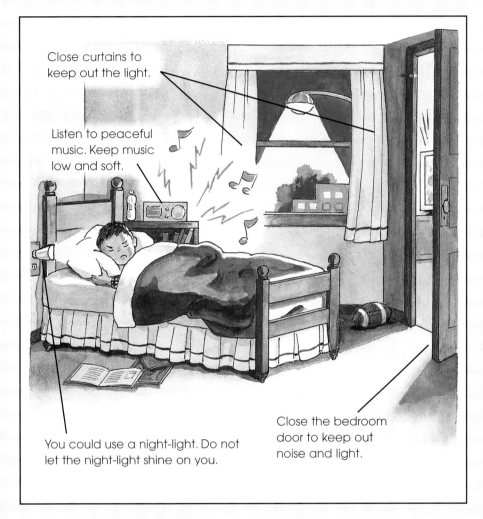

Close curtains to keep out the light.

Listen to peaceful music. Keep music low and soft.

You could use a night-light. Do not let the night-light shine on you.

Close the bedroom door to keep out noise and light.

Dream Catcher

Some people believe you can protect yourself from having bad dreams. Some Native Americans hang a "dream catcher" over their beds. Here's how to make your own dream catcher.

You will need:

- paper plate
- hole punch
- yarn (any color)
- large beads
- feathers
- safety scissors

1. Cut the center out of the paper plate. Ask an adult for help. Punch holes along the rim of the plate.

2. Make the web with a long piece of yarn. Tie one end of the yarn around one hole. Then, thread the yarn through all the holes. Make the yarn crisscross. This will make your web.

3. Cut three short pieces of yarn. Tie a feather to one end of each piece. String some beads on each piece. Tie each piece to a hole on one side of the plate.

4. Cut a long piece of yarn. Thread it through a hole at the top of the plate. Tie the ends of the yarn together. Make a loop.

5. Hang your dream catcher above your bed. Maybe it will help keep away bad dreams!

Word List

Challenging Words

beehive	gleam	prairie	succeed
breeze	peace	sixteen	

Decodable ea, ee, & ie Words

Allie	eagle	leak	street
beach	eat	leaves	sweet
beat	Ellie	peek	three
bees	feast	peep	tree
creak	feet	sea	weak
dreams	field	sleep	weep

High-Frequency Words

a	funny	look	the
an	get	love	their
and	go	make	then
are	good	my	there
around	have	night	they
as	help	not	this
at	house	now	to
back	I	o'clock	up
but	if	of	we
can	in	oh	what
did	is	on	will
do	it	our	you
don't	last	put	
find	let's	see	
found	little	sisters	